MYTH

RAIDERS

MYTH RAIDERS

MEDUSA'S CURSE

A. J. HUNTER

ILLUSTRATED BY JAMES DE LA RUE

LITTLE, BROWN BOOKS FOR YOUNG READERS
www.lbkids.co.uk

LITTLE, BROWN BOOKS FOR YOUNG READERS

First published in Great Britain in 2015 by
Hodder & Stoughton

A CIP catalogue record for this book
is available from the British Library.

ISBN: 978-0-349-12436-0

Typeset in Caslon by M Rules
Printed and bound in Great Britain by
Clays Ltd, St Ives plc

The paper and board used in this book are made
from wood from responsible sources.

MIX
Paper from
responsible sources
FSC
www.fsc.org   FSC® C104740

Little, Brown Books for Young Readers
An imprint of
Hachette Children's Group
Part of Hodder & Stoughton
Carmelite House
50 Victoria Embankment
London EC4Y 0DZ

An Hachette UK Company
www.hachette.co.uk

www.hachettechildrens.co.uk

CONTENTS

WHAT'S THE
WORST THAT
COULD HAPPEN?

"**H**it it!" yelled Trey, duck-
ing as the winged creature
swooped out of the cave, its
red eyes burning, claws swiping.

"What do you *think* I'm trying to do?"
hollered Sam, her voice swallowed up

by the monster's shrieks. She swung a broken branch. The creature flapped its leathery black wings, sending a putrid stench into their faces. Trey couldn't really believe that this was happening. It was *crazy*. Three seconds ago he and his cousin had been in his basement at home – now, they were halfway up a mountain, and under deadly attack from a flying monster.

He snatched up a stone and lobbed it at the creature. It made a satisfying *thunk* as it ricocheted off the back of the thing's small, hairless skull. "Ha! Take *that*!"

The creature twisted in the air, its vicious fangs extending from its mouth as it hurtled towards Trey. Its long, curved claws reached for his throat.

He stumbled backwards, tripping over the rocks and bones that were strewn around the mouth of the cave. He threw out an arm, grabbing a bone and flinging it at the winged creature that hovered over him like a red-eyed, drooling nightmare.

It was about four feet tall and looked more or less like a human female – except for the six-foot bat wings that sprouted from its shoulders. Its black skeletal frame was dressed in filthy rags that hung over its limbs like tattered cobwebs. It had a rat-like face, thin skin stretched over a small, pitted skull. Huge bloodshot eyes stared with evil intent. With every flap of its charred wings, a disgusting stench wafted down over him. Trey didn't know what death smelt like, but he guessed *this* could be it.

Just moments ago, he and Sam had been in the basement, gawping over the two halves of a prehistoric metal disc, wondering if they should put them together to see if they fit.

"What's the worst that could happen?" Sam had asked.

Well, *the worst* turned out to be a blinding flash and a deafening boom. They'd been thrown through time and space to a wide, dark cave mouth, with mountains towering into the blue sky and forested foothills stretching away below. There was a city of white stone buildings in the valley – a city that looked very, very old.

Don't think, you idiot – duck! Trey tried to dive to one side, but the monster's long skeletal fingers clamped down on his shoulders.

"Get your claws off him!" Sam yelled, swinging the branch. There was a crack as it made violent contact. The creature released Trey, hissing and spitting, extending its arms towards her. She only just managed to leap out of range as a set of razor claws raked the air.

Trey jumped up again, rocks and bone fragments rolling under his feet as he fought for balance. The thing was attacking Sam now. *Not if I can help it!*

He picked up a large chunk of bone, bigger than his fist and jaggedly sharp. Drawing his arm back like he was pitching a softball, Trey aimed at the side of the creature's skull. He hesitated. But the monster was going to hurt Sam – he couldn't let that happen.

Do it, he urged himself. *Come on!*

He flung the bone. It struck the creature on the cheek with a sickening crunch. The monster screamed, its claws coming up to its face. It wrapped its wings around its body as it crashed to the ground.

Sam darted forward, lifting the branch high and bringing it down with a *whoosh*. But their enemy squirmed aside at the last moment and the branch broke in half on the hard, stony ground.

"Owwww!" Sam yelped, jumping back and shaking her stinging hand.

"This is insane!" she shouted. "We have to get out of here!"

Trey saw how scared she was, but how could they escape from something with wings?

"Maybe we can drive it off!" he yelled, jumping up at a tree and tearing down a thick, gnarled branch. He ripped off leaves and twigs, before moving in on the crawling creature. He jabbed at it while Sam hunted around for another weapon.

The creature rose to its feet, with a shriek as piercing as a car slamming its brakes. At the same moment, a shape appeared at the cave entrance. It was another of the monsters, and its glaring red eyes were fixed on Sam.

"Sam, watch out!" Trey yelled. "There are two of them!"

His cousin spun towards the cave, looking panicked as the creature shot into the air and then swooped down at her. She flung herself on to her back and aimed a high kick at the monster.

Wham! Right in the gut!

Shrieking, the creature doubled up and went crashing into the trees.

"Gotcha!" Sam yelled, jumping back to her feet.

From behind them, the first creature let out a furious screeching. They spun around and saw its eyes burning with vengeance.

The craziness wasn't over yet.

Trey lunged forward, jamming the

branch into the monster's ribs, trying to drive it back into the cave. How many more of these things were in there? How could this be *real*?

The shrieking thing snatched at the branch and took to the air again. But instead of diving at Trey, it swerved sideways and reached out towards the metal disc that lay on the ground, glowing faintly.

It wants the disc.

Trey's mind whirled. He and Sam had arrived here moments after they put the two pieces of the disc together. Was *that* how they'd been zapped to this madhouse? Maybe that was the way home, too. Thinking quickly, he threw the branch aside and scooped up a rock, hurling it at the disc. It cracked on the circle of metal and bounced off. The two halves of the disc broke apart and spun through the air, one half smacking neatly into Trey's open palm, and the other sailing right into Sam's hand!

There was another bright flash, a second thunderous *boom*. Trey staggered, blinking as the light faded and the screams disappeared. He looked around. They were back in the basement of his family home.

With a stunned look, Sam sank heavily on to the concrete floor.

The two cousins stared at one another.

"What was *that*?" gasped Sam.

2

TOO WEIRD

THREE MONTHS BEFORE THE WORST HAPPENED

Beverly, Massachusetts

"Hey, Dad, take a look at this!" Thirteen-year-old Trey Wilson's small, wiry frame was folded up in the living room armchair, his feet on the cushion, his tablet on his bony knees. He pushed his dark, curly hair out of his eyes as he stared at the screen, his fingers tapping at the keyboard. Trey had been browsing eBay for interesting prehistoric and Neolithic material for his collection, and he'd just spotted something totally awesome.

"What is it, buddy?" His father, Dom, leaned over the back of the chair.

Trey pointed to the picture of a half-moon-shaped disc made of some brownish-grey metal. It was engraved all over with strange and unsettling symbols – Trey could make out pyramids and crossed swords, staring eyes, skulls, stars and a *lot* of bizarre animal heads, all jumbled up together. The whole thing looked weird and kind of ... well, *ominous*.

"That's pretty creepy," his father said, tousling Trey's hair. "I can see why it'd grab *your* attention."

Trey grinned. His dad was right – he did love freaky things! He jabbed a finger at the page. "They're saying it might be Bronze Age – or even earlier." He began to read. "'Ancient Ritual Pendant, Brazil. This artefact was discovered in the Barra de Guaratiba region of Rio de Janeiro. The other half of this disc is yet to be found. Although broken, it is a unique piece of ancient history.'" He twisted his head to look up at his father. "Can I buy it?"

His dad peered at the price tag. "Expensive," he said.

"That's because it's *unique*," Trey shot back.

His dad made a noise that was half-sigh, half-laugh. "Will your allowance cover it? Your mom'll break *me* in half if I have to loan you the difference."

Trey grinned at him. "I've been saving up for something for the last year."

Finally, his father nodded. "Go for it — just be sure to tell your mom it was on some kind of special offer."

Trey had clicked on "Buy It Now" almost before his father had finished speaking.

TWO WEEKS BEFORE THE
WORST HAPPENED

London

Samantha Wilson ran a hand through her spiky ash-blonde hair as she looked over a map of Angola, on the west coast of Africa – where she would *not* be going to join her mother on a research expedition. Instead, she was being packed off to spend the summer with her cousin Trey and his family in Massachusetts. She liked Trey – he was the same age as her and, as geeks went, he was pretty cool. They'd never actually met, but they'd been Skype buddies for the last two years, and email buddies for as long as Sam could remember before that.

But this summer, she'd really hoped to go with her mother. Instead, her mum had gone alone, leaving Sam to stay with her gran for a few days before her trip to America.

Then the parcel had arrived, post-marked "Luanda, Angola".

It had contained a flattish, carefully wrapped object and a note from her mum: "I really wish you could have come. Here's something I think you'll like – it's very, very, very old."

Intrigued, Sam had unwrapped the gift.

"Cool ... I, uh, *think* ... "

At first glance, the thing looked like half of a thick broken plate – made of a dull greyish-brown metal and covered all over with a tangled mass of engraved shapes. Sam stared in fascination at the triangles and skulls and long knives, stars, and a higgledy-piggledy collection of very odd-looking animals' heads. The disc felt strangely warm as she turned it over in her hands.

. . . very, very, very old . . .

It wasn't so much that it *looked* old, it was more that it *felt* old. Sam could imagine some skilled artist, thousands of years ago, hunched over the metal disc, carefully etching the intricate designs.

Trey was into weird old stuff, constantly emailing her links to articles about archaeological finds in far-off places. Now Sam grinned, starting to feel hopeful as she thought back to the half-disc. When she turned up on her cousin's doorstep with an ancient African artefact, he would go green – bright, glowing, radioactive green! Maybe this summer wouldn't be so bad after all …

TEN MINUTES BEFORE THE WORST HAPPENED

The basement of the Wilson house, Beverly, Massachusetts

"Wow!" Trey's jaw dropped as Sam took the brownish-grey half-disc out of the padded envelope.

The cousins sat facing each other, cross-legged on the concrete floor. "I knew you'd be impressed," Sam said, laying it carefully down between them. "Mum sent it to me from Angola. I bet even *you* haven't got anything like this in your collection."

Trey made a strangled noise in his throat, before bounding for the stairs, taking them three at a time.

"What's up?" Sam called after him.

"You'll see!" Trey yelled back.

He came back down, carrying his own half-disc.

"I got it on eBay," he told her breathlessly, as he sat back down in front of her with the disc in his hands. "It was found in Brazil."

He placed his half-disc on the floor close to Sam's. They leaned in. The engravings on the two halves looked as though the same person had carved them. The broken edges mirrored each other.

"Weird," murmured Trey. "One half was found in Africa, and the other in South America."

"And the whole Atlantic Ocean in between," breathed Sam. "How does that make sense?"

There was a pause, while Trey's eyes darted left and right. "But that's impossible," he blurted out.

"What is?"

Trey looked at her, eyes narrowed. "You ever heard of Gondwana?"

Sam frowned. "Wasn't it a gigantic continent that split up millions and millions of years ago? The different chunks slowly drifted apart, until they ended up the way they are now."

"That's right," said Trey. "It's all to do with tectonic plates. East Gondwana split from West Gondwana in the early part of the Jurassic period."

"So?"

Trey stared at her. "So, East Gondwana is now called Africa ..."

"And West Gondwana is South America," finished Sam. "I know, but what does that ...? *Oh* ..."

They stared at each other, and then down at the two halves of the disc — and then back at each other. Did these half-discs come from a huge land mass that had broken up and drifted apart 180 million years ago?

Sam spoke first. "Hold on, though . . . this thing was obviously made by a person – a human being – but there weren't any people around in the Jurassic period . . ."

Trey just nodded.

"So they *can't* be part of the same thing," said Sam. "Not unless the whole of human history is wrong."

Trey frowned. "They sure *look* like someone made them." He reached out and moved the two halves closer together, then paused, hesitating. "Does your half always feel warm?"

Sam nodded.

"Mine, too," said Trey. He looked up at his cousin. "What if the two halves fit?"

Sam glanced at the pieces, and the rough, ragged edges. She shrugged.

"Let's try it out," she said. "What's the worst that could happen?"

3

LORD OF THE LIGHT

JUST AFTER THE WORST HAPPENED

The cousins were back in the basement. Breathless. Shocked. Confused. "What was *that*?" gasped Sam.

Trey gaped at her. "How should I know?"

He stared down at the half of the disc in his hand. "It's stopped glowing," he said in a low voice.

"But is it still warm?" asked Sam, peering at the half disc in her own hand. "Mine is."

Trey nodded. "The glow stopped when they came apart. What's that all about?"

"Don't ask me." Sam blew her cheeks out. "It was pretty amazing, wasn't it? I mean – *wow!*"

"One thing's for sure," Trey said. "We have to keep the two halves as far apart as we can."

"No way," said Sam. "We should put

them together and see if we get sent to that weird place again." She turned her half-disc over in her hands, examining it from all sides.

Trey hid the first piece behind his back. "You are *not* putting them together again," he said firmly. "Not without taking proper precautions."

"Fine," she said. "What precautions did you have in mind?"

Trey's brain whizzed. A lead-lined nuclear bunker in the middle of the Mojave Desert. Him at least a hundred miles away. Wearing a hazmat suit.

Sam sprang forward and whipped the disc out from behind him. Before Trey could react, she slammed the two halves together like she was playing cymbals in an orchestra.

"Sam, don't!" he yelled, reaching for the disc. She backed away from him, her body tensing and jerking. Her head whipped from side to side, her teeth clenched as though in agony. Her arms thrust forward, the two halves of the disc glowing faintly in her hands as they had before. "*Sam!*"

Her body relaxed and she grinned wickedly at him over the rim of the disc. "Joking!" she said. "Look. It's fine. We're still here, aren't we?"

Trey glanced anxiously around, as if he half-expected to find a yawning cave mouth right behind him.

"But it's doing that glowy thing

again," he said. "What if . . ."

A sudden rushing sound filled the basement, as though a tornado was ripping through it. A bright white light erupted near the stairs. A voice roared from its intense, burning heart.

" . . . *until the Lords of the Dark might return.*"

The light faded to reveal . . . a man. He was tall and pale, with a fierce, hawk-like face framed by long, silvery hair. His billowing white cloak swept the floor, looking just like a monk's habit, and caught at the waist by a silver band.

The two cousins stared at him as he staggered, supporting himself against the wall, before righting himself and gazing at them with deep-set, silver-grey eyes.

"The Chosen Ones!" he said in a deep voice. "I have answered your call. What damage have the Lords of the Dark done? Is there a glimmer of Light still in the world?"

"Who are you?" Trey asked shakily.

"I am Michael Kyrios Lux, first Lord of the Light," said the man, his voice now sounding normal. Well, not *normal*-normal, but definitely less otherworldly.

"OK, Mr Lux," blurted Sam. "I think what we really want to know is *what* you are, and how you got here?" She glared at him. "Hey – were those

bird-women anything to do with you? Because if they were . . . "

Michael raised his hand. "You speak too fast," he said. "My mind reels. I do not understand your questions."

Sam and Trey exchanged a confused look. "Are you . . ." Trey gulped, "like . . . an archangel?"

Michael frowned, as if the word meant nothing to him.

"Or a wizard?" suggested Sam. "A magician? You know – hocus-pocus and all that? Or are you from the future – with a time machine?"

"Your words are unknown to me," said Michael. "But, since my last visit to this world, labels for my kind may have changed." He looked them both up and down. He held his fingertips to his fore-head, screwing his eyes tight shut. Then his eyes snapped open and he let out a breath. "I did not expect the Chosen Ones to be children, but Destiny is not to be questioned. You have called me and I have come."

Chosen Ones? So much for sense!

Sam elbowed her cousin. "Have you noticed his hair and clothes?" she whispered. "Is that weird, or what?"

Trey *had* noticed. Michael's clothes were rippling and his hair was stream-ing out to one side as though he were standing in a fierce wind – except there wasn't even the faintest breath of air down in the basement.

"Uh … we didn't … *call* you …"

stammered Trey. "I think, uh ... you've come to the ... wrong place ..."

Michael pointed to the disc in Sam's hands. "You have reunited the Heart of Light," he said. "Why would you do that, if not to summon me as your guide?"

"We didn't mean to summon a guide," said Sam. "We were just ..." she glanced sideways at Trey, " ... messing around ..."

"Yeah, it was a total accident," he added. "We're not the *Chosen Ones* at all." He gave Michael a rueful look. "It's all been a huge mistake. Sorry."

Michael's white teeth flashed as he laughed. "Chosen Ones, there are no mistakes. Destiny has brought the three of us together." His smile faded and he folded his arms, his robe still rippling. "Don't you understand? The fate of the world rests upon your shoulders."

4

THE CHOSEN ONES

The two cousins gazed at Michael in stunned disbelief. Nothing he said made any kind of sense.

"Why is your hair doing that?" Sam asked eventually.

His face was expressionless. "I must travel at great speed to keep up with this world as it plunges headlong through the Universe."

Sam blinked. "Oh. I see." She didn't see at all.

"I think I know what's going on," said Trey. "The earth spins on its axis at about one thousand miles per hour. And it moves around the sun at about sixty-seven thousand miles per hour." He swallowed hard as he looked at Sam. "I think Michael comes from somewhere, uh . . . more *stationary*, you know? It's like if one of us jumped on to a moving carousel – that was going really, *really* fast."

"Of course," said Sam blankly. "It's totally obvious when you think about it." She gazed at Michael. "The last time we put the two halves of the … uh … Heart of Light together, did we get sent to the same place you come from?"

"No," said Michael. "You travelled back through time and space in your own world."

"Oh, is *that* what happened?" Sam said heavily. "Fine, then. No problem."

"Destiny has chosen the two of you to gather the scattered pieces of the Warrior's Shield so that you may defend this world against the attack of the Dark."

Sam folded her arms. "You're going to have to explain it better than that."

"What's the Dark?" Trey added. "And why is it going to attack us? What did *we* do?"

Michael looked keenly from one to the other. "There have been many battles between the forces of Light and Dark over the long aeons of this world's existence," he said grimly. "The last battle took place long, long ago. It was hard, but we did our duty and we could rest, knowing this world was safe . . . for the time being."

"And now it's not safe any more?" asked Sam uneasily.

"It is not," said Michael. "The Dark is coming again – your world must be defended, the Warrior's Shield must be made whole again. The Chosen

Ones must seek its fragments from the mythic times."

"Mythic times?" Sam said hesitantly. "Excuse me, but the whole point about myths is that they're ... *mythical*. Like, made up."

"Are you saying that all the things we think of as being mythical are actually real?" asked Trey.

"I am," said Michael.

"And how exactly do we get into these mythic times?" asked Sam.

"The Heart of Light is the very centre of the shield, and it will be your portal into the past – when you each hold one half," said Michael. "As you travel, you will find the other fragments of the Warrior's Shield. You will gather them and bring them back here where they will be reunited."

"Can I just stop you there?" Trey said, his hand pressed against his head. "Three questions. How many bits was the shield broken into? How much time do we have to find them? And what exactly will the Dark do?"

Michael's eyes glowed, as though he was seeing far-off things. "There are four pieces that you must find," he said solemnly. "The Dark is coming. It will strike the earth at midnight in four days' time, beating upon your world like a mighty hammer. Nothing will survive, save a scattering of barren and broken rock circling your sun for all eternity."

There was a long pause while the cousins tried to take this in.

"Four days, four pieces of shield," said Sam at last, shaking her head. "That's cutting it a bit fine." When she couldn't bear the silence any more, she turned to face Trey. "Looks like we're the Chosen Ones. So we'd better suit up and get ready to save the world."

Trey swallowed hard. He turned to Michael. "You're going to have to give us a whole lot more information," he croaked, his heart hammering.

But Michael didn't seem to hear him. He was standing stiffly, his hands balled into fists at his sides, his silvery eyes staring over their heads.

"I think he's out of it for the moment," said Sam, waving her hand in front of Michael's unseeing eyes.

"But what do you think he means by 'mythic times'?" Trey murmured. "Which 'mythic times'? Where? And when?"

Sam shrugged. "Every country in the world has its own myths, doesn't it?" she said. "Maybe we'll get sent to Ancient Greece. Hey, we might get to meet Thor."

"That's *Norse* mythology," said Trey. "Not Greek."

"OK, Greek geek. What I'm saying is, this could be kind of awesome." She grinned. "And to think, I was disappointed about not getting to go to Angola – but we could wind up on Mount Olympus!"

Trey gave a sarcastic thumbs up. "Yay! And we could get stomped to mush by the Titans. Or be ripped into tiny shreds by . . . " He paused, his eyes widening. "I know what those flying things were . . . They were harpies!"

"You are correct, Chosen One." They turned at the sound of Michael's voice. He seemed to have come out of his trance. "You will go back in time two and a half thousand years to the land of Greece," he said. "The fragment of the Warrior's Shield lies deep in a cave upon a high mountainside."

"Oh great," said Sam. "The same cave those harpy things came out of, I bet."

"The harpies are servants," said Michael, raising his hand in a warning gesture. "They serve an ancient creature. Beware their mistress, Chosen Ones . . . beware the serpent woman!"

5

RESEARCH MODE

"Two packets of potato chips, two candy bars, two cans of soda, two bottles of water." Trey peered into the open mouth of his backpack as he recited its contents. "Two LED flashlights. A penknife. A compass. One first-aid kit – just in case." He looked up at

Sam. "Anything else you can think of?"

"A couple of grenades would be nice," she said.

"Sorry, Mom confiscated my grenades after the incident with the next-door neighbour's cat."

Sam rolled her eyes. "Ha, ha, very funny. Then I guess we're sorted," she said.

They were in Trey's bedroom, speed-prepping for their trip to Ancient Greece.

They had left Michael on his own in the basement. Trey just prayed that his mom didn't decide she needed something from down there.

"Are we out of our minds?" Trey

asked, zipping up the backpack. "I mean – seriously?"

"Totally," Sam reassured him.

He frowned, grabbing his tablet from the nightstand. "I'm just going to Google *harpies*, really quickly," he muttered. "We may as well find out everything we can about them."

He clicked to open a page. There was a line drawing of a winged harpy that didn't look anything like as horrible as the things they had encountered.

He began to read: "'The harpies of Greek myth were originally thought to be beautiful winged maidens—'"

"Sure – if rabid coyotes are your thing!" said Sam.

"' ... but later, they were depicted

as hideous monsters equipped with crooked, sharp talons and fangs—'" Trey continued.

"Does it mention that they look like something that's been left in the oven way too long?" Sam asked.

Trey read on. "'Their role in mythology was to carry people off to the Underworld and punish them with cruel torments and anguishes. In some tales, they were the protectors of a great secret, and would rend apart anyone who dared approach their lair.'"

"What kind of 'great secret'?" said Sam. "Would a piece of the Warrior's Shield count?"

Trey nodded. "I bet it would," he said. He looked into her eyes. "This is going to be really dangerous, you do get that, don't you?"

"Here's the thing," Sam replied. "Michael told us we were the Chosen Ones, right?"

"That's what he *said*," Trey admitted. "But he could be wrong. My mom *says* I'm the most handsome boy in all the world."

"No offence, cuz, but your mother's off her head," said Sam. "The point is, Michael is not Mr Normal, from Normaltown, Normalia, is he? He's some kind of ..." She paused, groping for words. "He's *different*, OK? He's a super-being of some kind. He *knows* stuff. Unbelievable stuff – crazy, off-the-scale-mental, weird stuff."

"Your point being?" asked Trey.

"We're the Chosen Ones, with the fate of the world resting on our shoulders," Sam explained. "Michael's hardly going to let us get chewed up and spat out by a bunch of harpies on our first mission."

Trey took a long, deep breath. "OK," he said finally. "Let's get back down there and do it." He stopped suddenly, a thought hitting him. "Michael said the Dark's first attack would come at midnight in four days' time, right?"

"He did," agreed Sam, heading for the door. "So we'd better get moving."

"There's a meteor shower due in four days' time," Trey said. "Don't you remember? My dad's going to take us up to the top of Hawkeye Ridge with the telescope after sundown to watch it."

"That's *this* week?" said Sam, her eyes widening. "Whoa! Freaky!"

A meteor shower visible over New England in four nights' time.

The first attack of the Dark – due to strike at midnight the same night.

Two Chosen Ones tasked with saving the world.

None of this felt like a coincidence.

Michael was standing exactly as they had left him, stiff and upright.

"Are you ready, Chosen Ones?" he

asked. Trey noticed that he was holding the two halves of the ancient disc – one in each hand.

"As we'll ever be," said Sam.

"It's the meteor shower, isn't it?" blurted Trey. "That's how the Dark is going to hit us."

"That is correct," said Michael. "There is no more time for speech. Here, take the Heart of Light."

He handed each of them a half.

"So, what's the plan?" Sam asked, feeling that familiar but unsettling warmth seeping through her skin as she held her half of the disc.

"The task is for you to determine," said Michael. "You are the Chosen Ones."

"There's no plan?" said Trey in alarm. "Then, you have to come with us. We can't do this on our own."

"I am not permitted," said Michael. "I can only guide you to the path – how you walk it is not for me to decide. But I can do one thing more for you." He raised his hand. A ball of fluffy blue-white light floated from his palm. It divided in two and glided towards the cousins, sinking softly into their chests without any sensation.

"That was weird," said Sam, touching her chest.

"What *was* that?" asked Trey.

"It is a glamour that will allow you to understand and be understood in any language wherever you go," Michael explained. "Farewell, Chosen Ones. I will await your return."

"Hold everything," said Trey. "Last time we put the disc together, we landed right outside the harpies' cave. We only just survived."

"Chill, cuz," said Sam. "It'll be fine. Like I told you before, Michael knows what he's doing." She looked at their guide, his impenetrable eyes fixed on them. "We'll take a trip into the past, kick some harpy butt, grab the piece of the shield and be back here in time for dinner. Isn't that right, Michael?" He didn't say a word. Sam gave a shaky smile. "Trust me, Trey. It's going to be awesome!" Then she slammed her half of the disc against his.

6

INTO THE
MYTHIC TIMES

It felt as if they'd brought together the bare ends of live electric cables. There was a loud crackling, fizzing noise and a flash of brilliant blue-white light.

Trey staggered back, covering his eyes with his hands, aware of the disc slipping from his fingers.

He heard Sam's voice. "Wow!"

He took his hands away from his face, blinking as his surroundings gradually became clear.

They were back outside the cave. Mountains towered above. Forests stretched below.

Trey ducked, expecting harpies to come soaring down out of the sky. His heart was beating so hard and fast that it felt like his skull was full of drumming.

"Quick, this way!" Sam grabbed his collar and hauled him across the bone-strewn ground. Stumbling, he almost fell on top of her as she dived for cover behind a heap of boulders.

"Where ... are ... the ... harpies?" he

panted, fighting for breath, trying hard to gather his scattered wits. "I thought they'd be all over us."

"Maybe it's their nap time," said Sam, peering over the top of the boulders.

The branches of an olive tree hung above their heads, throwing heavy shadows over them and filling the air with an exotic scent. Insects buzzed in the hot, dry air.

Cautiously, Trey lifted his head above the boulders. More olive trees grew among the rocks and stones that scattered the small mountain plateau, their tangled roots digging fiercely into the ground, their branches twisted like gnarled fingers clawing the air.

Beyond the stony ridge, the mountain fell rapidly away in forested slopes, brown rocks jutting out like broken bones. There were more mountains on the horizon, hazy blue under the burning sun.

Trey's eyes were drawn to the cave, set back into the grey-brown mountainside, its entrance stretched wide like a gaping mouth. Light only bled a little way inside before it gave way to deep, dreadful darkness.

He hoped that wasn't some kind of *omen*.

"Look at all those bones," murmured Sam, pointing at the white shapes on the ground in front of the cave. "Know what? I'm not sure they're all animals."

She pointed to a single sandal, lying in the dirt, stained with splotches of something that could have been dried blood.

Trey scanned the bones. Some of them looked horribly like they might be human – long leg bones and broken ribcages. And a skull! Bleached white in the heat, its empty eye sockets staring right at them.

"People, for sure," he murmured. A worrying thought struck him. "Where's the Heart of Light?" he asked. "Shouldn't we keep it in the backpack?"

Sam shook her head. "We might lose the backpack," she said, lifting her T-shirt and showing him the disc tucked into the belt of her jeans. "I prefer it right here, where I know it's safe and sound." She raised an eyebrow. "So, how are we going to do this?" She was staring at the cave mouth. "Do you think the piece of the Warrior's Shield is in there?"

"Why are you asking me?" he said. "I have no idea. And even if those harpies are gone, what about that serpent woman Michael warned us about?"

"Tricky," agreed Sam. "I'm going to have a quick look about." Before Trey could move to join her, she crawled away from him along the line of boulders and towards the frowning cliff.

"Be careful!" Trey hissed after her.

Sam slipped over the boulders, hugging the mountainside as she made her way towards the cave mouth. Foul air wafted out of the cave. She wrinkled her nose. Phew!

Now that she was closer to the yawning darkness, she saw that there were rags and shreds of torn clothing among the bones. The harpies ate people. And

Michael had sent them here without any kind of weapons. How were they meant to defend themselves if those horrible things came back?

"We're the Chosen Ones," she murmered reassuringly to herself. "We'll find a way."

She was only one step from the cave mouth when she saw something from the corner of her eye. A dark fleck flying above the trees on wide leathery wings. It was a harpy, but it wasn't looking at her – it was staring at something further down the mountain.

There was a scrabbling sound from the cave and Sam ran to hide behind a rock. A few moments later, five other harpies burst out, yelling and howling.

"Hey – what just happened?" hissed a voice. It was Trey. He'd scrambled over to join her. "Something's spooked the harpies."

As his words faded away, another sound replaced them – the *clip-clop* of hooves. It was coming from further down the mountainside, where the first harpy had been staring.

On the far side of the plateau, the ground dipped between hulking shoulders of rock – forming a kind of natural walled pathway downwards.

The sound echoed around the mountain again.

Clip-clop. Clip-clop.

Hooves. Hooves on hard ground. Coming closer up the path.

Suddenly, a spear sailed through the air and a voice rang out.

"Winged filth! I come here to defeat you! I am Faunus, son of Silenus!" The spear pierced the ground a fraction from where the startled harpies were gathered. Then, the most amazing figure Sam had ever seen came charging into view.

7

THE SATYR AND
THE SNAKES

The rampaging figure was about a foot taller than Trey. It was olive-skinned and bare-chested, with a head of shiny, tangled black hair. Sharp, curling horns sprouted from the hair at either temple. The creature had burning amber eyes set in a face that was fierce and wild. Sam gawped in disbelief. From the waist down, the hair on the creature's body changed to the fur of an animal, and its great, powerful legs were exactly like a goat's.

"It's a satyr," Trey gasped. "I've seen pictures. Oh, wow! *They* really exist, too."

The satyr's shining hooves pounded on the baked earth as it hurtled forward, its mouth wide, lips drawn back from ferocious teeth.

The harpies rose in a flurry of dust, their wings spreading as they hovered in the air, staring down at the astonishing creature. Their eyes were red with rage, and their mouths hung open, dripping bloody saliva.

The satyr snatched up its spear and brandished it in the air.

"Winged filth!" he roared. "Come to me! I will wear your wings as a cloak! I will drink red wine from your skulls! I will make a necklace of your teeth! I will—"

A chorus of screams and screeches from the harpies drowned his next threat. They plunged down at him, mouths stretched wide, claws groping, their wings blurring as they swooped.

A claw ripped the spear from the satyr's fist and Sam saw a look of alarm come over his face as he disappeared beneath a wild flurry of wings and claws and teeth.

"We've got to help him!" yelled Sam,

leaping to her feet. "There are too many of them. They'll kill him!"

Trey was only half a step behind her as they vaulted over the boulder and raced forward. They both scooped up rocks and bone fragments, hurling them at the flapping mass of harpies.

"Get away from him, you brutes!" Sam howled.

As the first missiles struck home, a couple of harpies turned at the sudden pain. Their red eyes burned as they glared at Sam and Trey.

"Now we've done it!" gasped Trey as two harpies broke from the fray and came hurtling towards them. Shrieking. Red-eyed. All claws and fangs.

As Sam darted sideways from a slashing claw, Trey had to fling himself on to the ground to avoid a set of talons that raked his shoulders. He rolled over and over, his hair ruffled by a putrid gust as the harpy passed dangerously close to him.

A deep shadow fell over him as the harpy moved in for the kill. But the satyr's spear was within reach. He snatched it up and leapt to his feet. "Get lost!" he cried, stabbing at the harpy. "We're the Chosen Ones!" Screeching, the monster rose out of reach, spraying Trey's face with blood-streaked spittle.

Score one for Trey!

Sam dived into a forward roll, tucking

her head under and bringing her legs up in a powerful two-footed kick to the nearest harpy's stomach. *Crunch!* The harpy spun in an uncontrolled, looping arc, crashing to the ground in a tangle of wings.

Sam bounded to her feet, sweeping up a long bone in each hand. Trey was fending off another of the harpies with the satyr's spear. The rest were attacking the creature and Sam could see glimpses of his kicking hooves as they swarmed over him.

She rushed to help Trey, but a sudden movement from the cave mouth startled her and she spun around. Something was writhing through the air towards her. Scaled. Glistening. Sleek. Black-eyed. Wide mouths, forked tongues flicking, needle-sharp fangs protruding.

"Snakes!" Sam yelled. "Flying snakes!"

Trey had managed to escape his attacker. He edged towards where the satyr was still battling with the remaining harpies. He was almost there when the snakes came at him.

"Watch out!" Sam cried, but it was too late. One gaping mouth closed on the shaft of his spear. A slimy, slithery body coiled itself around his wrist. A set of fangs flew into his face.

In his panic, he remembered Michael's warning.

Beware the serpent woman.

He jerked his head back, punching fiercely at the snake coming for his face. It fell to the ground, writhing, but another was still coiled around his wrist. The fallen snake snapped viciously at the spear shaft he was holding, breaking it in two. Trey tripped, falling heavily, the breath beaten out of his lungs.

Sam launched one of the long bones at the snakes. It struck the leader in the face, sending it spinning off, spitting blood. She gripped the other bone in both hands and planted her feet firmly.

"Bring it on!" she yelled, swinging with the bone. She heard a *thwack* as bone struck scales and the snake fell to the ground. It thrashed for a few moments like a coil of wire, then it stopped moving.

One down!

She drew her hands up and cracked the end of the bone against a snake skull, knocking it out of the air. Adrenaline pumped through her as she fought. Sweat poured into her eyes, but she ignored its sting, and the ache of her muscles. She was a Chosen One! Trey ran to her side and waved what remained of his broken staff.

"We can do this!" she panted. She'd never been so glad to have her cousin by her side.

She yelled and swung her bone, fighting off snake after snake until she could hardly lift her arms. She saw Trey swipe at the last snake, then drop his staff, his chest heaving. There were no more – they'd defeated them! And the harpies had fled. Sam stared at the ground in a daze and made a rapid count. Seven snakes. All dead.

"Way to go, Chosen Ones!" gasped Trey. They gave each other a weary high five and turned away from the cave, ready to help the embattled satyr.

Turning their backs was a mistake.

8

UNLIKELY SAVIOURS

A sudden, furious hissing sound rose into the air. The sound of ...

"They've come back to life!" Trey cried, swivelling round. The snakes slithered over the ground, jaws open wide. One of the larger snakes leapt into the air, its fat body writhing as needle-sharp teeth aimed towards Sam's throat. Jets of poison shot from its mouth.

She whirled her bone through the air and it connected with the snake. It jolted and hissed with pain but wrapped its body around the weapon. Sam felt the snake's tail tighten on her wrist, and she quickly threw the bone away. The snake slithered in the dust.

Beside her, Trey was jumping from side to side, avoiding the mass of snakes that writhed around his feet. He swung his broken staff like a golf club, sending them flying through the air. They couldn't keep fighting like this! Sam could feel her whole body trembling with the effort. How long would it be before a set of jaws punctured her skin? She didn't want to die in Ancient Greece!

Then, she heard the strangest thing.

Tan-tarra-tarra!

Trumpets, ringing through the air.

Tan-tarra-tarra-tan-tarra!

The snakes broke off the attack. Squirming bodies went flying into the cave, their panicky hissing swallowed up in the darkness.

Sam dropped to her knees, giddy with pain and exhaustion and relief. She wiped the sweat out of her eyes and peered down the sunken path.

Satyrs. Seven? Eight? Nine? No, *ten* satyrs, charging up the path towards them. Huge, bearded satyrs, much taller and broader than the first one.

She staggered to her feet. "Trey! We're saved!"

The leading satyr came to a halt in front of her. Sam breathed hard through clenched teeth as she stared up at him.

He was a whole head taller than her. Great curved horns stabbed their way through the tangled mess of his reddish-brown hair. His eyes were like two deep pools of liquid amber, set in a grim face with a thick, curled beard.

The other satyrs gathered behind him, some carrying curved trumpets made of horn, others with spears in their fists. All bearded, all staring at her with fierce amber eyes.

"Thank you," Sam gasped. "You saved our lives."

"Wretched human!" snarled the first satyr, raising his spear in a sudden burst of movement. Sam froze to the spot as he grimaced at her. "You are in league with the winged filth! You have killed Faunus!"

"We were trying to *help* him!" Sam protested. "There were all these harpies and snakes and . . . it was *crazy*! But we were fighting on his side."

"Nikandros, Faunus is alive!" one of the satyrs cried, crouching over the fallen creature. "He is not badly hurt –

but his wits are wandering along the banks of the Styx."

Trey guessed he meant Faunus was unconscious. He glared at Nikandros.

"She's telling you the truth," he said. "The harpies attacked us as well."

Nikandros shifted the spear in his fist, his face grim. *He could do a lot of damage with that*, Trey thought.

He looked into Nikandros's savage, inhuman eyes. The big satyr still held the spear aloft, poised in the moment before the killing thrust. Trey needed to do something. Faunus had said he was the son of . . .

Got it!

"Silenus won't be pleased if you kill the two people who saved his son's life!"

Trey blurted, hoping he sounded more sure of himself than he felt. He stabbed a finger at the two satyrs who were dragging the unconscious Faunus to his feet, supporting him between them as his head lolled. "What are you going to say when Faunus wakes up and tells his father what really happened? You are going to be in so much trouble!"

Nikandros eyed Trey thoughtfully for a few moments, then his spear-arm dropped. Another of the satyrs came to his side.

"You know how Faunus likes to dream of defeating the harpies," he whispered in his leader's ear. "He has all the foolish fire of youth."

Nikandros nodded, grimly. "That is true, Pavlos," he muttered. He looked at the cousins. "Perhaps you are not allied with the winged filth." His voice was rough and raspy, like a rusty sword scraping wet stone. "But what is your purpose on our mountain?"

Trey and Sam shared another glance. Oh, wow! What should they tell him?

The truth?

Seriously?

"The harpies have something we need," Trey said hesitantly. "We were trying to get it back."

"Humans do not come on to the mountain," said Nikandros. "They live in their city." He stamped the heel of his spear on the ground. "Humans can never come here! This is *our* realm."

Holding Nikandros's gaze was like

making eye contact with a tiger.

"You are not welcome here. Your place is with the rest of your kind." The air pulsed with threat. Nikandros reached out a hand and placed it on Trey's shoulder, gripping hard. Trey tried not to tremble – much. "But first, come back with us. Explain yourselves to our lord. If you have spoken the truth, you will be praised for saving his son's life. If not ..." He turned to the satyrs, bunched silently at his back. "Nandros, Pavlos, lead the way."

Trey retrieved his backpack from where it had fallen in the dirt during the battle. He hefted it on to his back. Sam came to stand beside him. Her face was white.

Together, they followed anxiously as Nikandros led the strange troop down the mountain path, with two satyrs supporting Faunus. Trey had to admit, it would be good to have a break from fighting.

He stared at the hairy goat legs of the satyrs, stamping along ahead of him. Their curling horns glinted in the light.

If we get out of Ancient Greece in one piece, I'm going to have the most epic *stories to tell at school next semester!* he thought, trying to lift his spirits. But would anyone believe him?

9

TRAPPED!

s they descended, the dirt track ran steeply down into thick forests. But Nikandros led them away from the path, through a tumbled, stony landscape of olive trees and scrub. Trey was exhausted and he ached like he'd just run a marathon.

At last, they came out of the trees and

on to a ledge of brown stone, staring out over a stunning view of forested mountains and deep valleys under a wide blue sky.

"Your city lies below!" said Nikandros, standing on the lip of the ledge and beckoning Trey forward. It wasn't their city, but Trey wasn't sure now was the time to say so.

He stood at the satyr's side and peered gingerly over the edge. He caught his breath. He wasn't particularly scared of heights, but the sheer giddying drop took him by surprise. Sam came to stand beside him. Her face still looked pale and as she gazed over the precipice she shuddered.

"That's a long way down," she said

faintly. Way, way below, the city nestled under the high cliff, its sun-baked white buildings like toys. It had to be four hundred feet straight down from where they were standing.

"Are you all right?" Trey asked. His cousin was usually so brave and cheerful – he'd never seen her looking like this before. She rubbed a hand across her forehead and gave herself a shake. "I'm fine," she said with a weak smile. "Never better."

"Once you've rested, you will be sent back to your own kind," snapped a voice behind them. Nikandros. Suddenly, he grasped Trey and Sam and drew them to him. "And you will *never* come back, unless ..." He let

his threat go unspoken, as he gripped their arms – hard. Trey gasped in pain, and saw that Sam was trying to prise herself free.

"Nikandros – in my father's name, let those humans go!" Faunus had been propped unconscious against a tree trunk at the back of the ledge. But his eyes were open now, and his hand was stretched out towards them.

Nikandros loosened his hold on the cousins. At the same time Sam tried to pull herself free, but as she heaved back, she lost her balance. She snatched for Trey but her fingers missed. She crashed heavily to the ground, her head striking the stone with a sharp crack.

Trey ran towards his cousin.

"You humans should never have set foot up here," Nikandros snarled.

"They came to my aid!" Faunus declared angrily, helping Trey lift Sam up. Her eyes were closed and there was a trickle of blood at her temple. *This is worse than I could ever have imagined*, Trey thought. *Can we just go home now, please?* But he knew that without Sam conscious enough to hold her own part of the disc, they were both trapped in Ancient Greece – with harpies, snakes and a large, dangerous satyr who seemed to hate them.

"These children should be rewarded for their courage," Faunus exclaimed. *If Sam was awake she'd say something like, "We're not children! We're the Chosen*

Ones!" thought Trey. But she was *not* awake. The weight of her body lay heavily in his arms.

Nikandros's grim face clenched in a deep frown. "Why did you put yourself at risk of Medusa's Curse, Faunus, when you know it is forbidden to approach her cave?"

Faunus's amber eyes flashed defiance. "I do not answer to you for my actions, Nikandros. I answer only to my father."

"And so you shall," Nikandros rumbled.

Medusa's Curse? Trey thought, his mind swirling. *What's that all about?* Medusa was the gorgon with the snakes for hair and a face so ugly it turned people to stone.

Trey could have slapped himself. *'Beware the serpent woman,'* Michael had told them. How could they have been so *dumb* that they hadn't figured it out? They were in mythic times. The serpent woman was Medusa. The *actual* Medusa! And she was up in that cave, guarding the piece of the Warrior's Shield.

"Have no fear, human," said Faunus, bursting into Trey's thoughts and resting his heavy brown hand on his shoulder. "We shall take you and your friend back to the Emerald Glade. Her injuries will be treated and you can rest. I will ask Silenus to pardon you for your transgressions in coming up our mountain. Come."

"I just want Sam to be OK," Trey

said, looking down into his cousin's face. He suddenly found it very difficult to care about the Warrior's Shield.

Two of the satyrs came and took her from him and carried her body between them. They pushed on down the rocky mountainside, passing through the spindly groves of olive trees. Eventually, they came to a place where trees soared above them, their wide canopies throwing down a deep, scented shade.

Trey found the climb down the steep mountainside sheer torture after the exhausting and painful battle with the harpies and the snakes. He could hardly keep up with the satyrs as they leapt nimbly downwards, their goats' hooves sure-footed on the treacherous slopes.

Finally, they arrived at a dense archway of trees, sweet-smelling jasmine creeping along the branches. Trey could hear the faint sound of music from beyond the vegetation.

Faunus turned and smiled, drawing back a branch. "Do not fear," he said. "My father is wise and gracious. He will do you no harm."

10

THE EMERALD GLADE

Faunus led them into an open area filled with bright sunlight. It took Trey a few moments to get the dazzle out of his eyes after the gloom of the forest. But as he took in his surroundings, his jaw dropped and his legs almost gave under him.

They were in a wide, grassy clearing filled with music and laughter and the bright sound of falling water. At the far side of the clearing a tumble of white rocks spilt bubbling streams down into a circular pool. Satyrs sat on rocks around the pool's rim – male and female, full-grown and children. Some wore flowers in their hair, and others had garlands of blossom around their necks and waists and wrists.

More satyrs danced in rings, their hooves skipping to the music of pipes and harps and hand drums. The walls of the glade hung with clusters of white and purple grapes, their scent filling Trey's head and making him dizzy.

But as Faunus led Trey into the glade, with Sam carried close behind them, the laughter and the dance ended abruptly. The music died away and a host of curious and anxious eyes stared at them.

"Come." Faunus beckoned Trey forward.

In a daze, Trey allowed himself to be guided across the clearing. He could feel the eyes following him. Small satyr children whimpered as he passed and their mothers clasped them tight.

They were afraid of *him*!

He and Faunus approached a large, ornate chair, constructed from living branches twisted and twined together and set back in a kind of arbour. Grapes and figs hung from the canopy of leaves and a chunky male Satyr with a massive belly half-sat, half-sprawled in the hammock-like seat. Others stood or sat around him, holding wooden bowls of fruit and cups of yellow liquid.

"Silenus, my father, I come to seek your pardon for my folly and to ask forgiveness for these wayward humans," said Faunus, bowing in front of the heavy-eyed satyr. "I went up the forbidden path and sought to do battle with the winged filth." His voice was full of remorse. "I was outmatched by their strength, and I would have been killed if these two humans had not come to my aid."

Silenus pulled himself upright and peered at Trey. He glanced past him at Sam, who had been laid on the ground. A satyr bent over her, pressing some moss against her wound. Another held a goblet to her lips.

"My cousin is badly hurt," Trey said, his voice croaking in his dry mouth. "Will she be OK?"

"Her wounds will be tended and she will be fed the tea of the Titans," Silenus said, eyeing Trey calmly. "Do not fear for her." He gestured towards Sam. "See, she awakens."

Trey could hardly believe it as Sam's eyes flicked open and she leapt to her feet as though she'd woken from a refreshing sleep.

"Interesting place," she said brightly, gazing around. Trey stared as his cousin jogged over to the throne. She looked so much better! And so quickly. Apart from a red-raw crescent-shaped cut above her left eyebrow, she seemed absolutely fine.

"Hi there," she said, grinning at Trey. "What's been happening?"

"Are you all right?" he gasped.

"I'm good," she shrugged. "Apart from a bit of a headache," she added, glaring at Nikandros.

"Come here, child," said Silenus.

Sam walked up to him, her arms folded, looking him right in the face. "My name's Sam and I'm a Chosen

One," she said. Trey tried not to smile – Sam was back, for sure, but she was also in danger of getting them into all kinds of trouble!

"He's Silenus," he hissed, edging up beside her. "The lord of the satyrs."

Silenus leaned forward, staring thoughtfully into Sam's face. He reached out and traced the curve of her wound with his fingertip. "You bear the mark of Light, child," he said. Then he leaned back and looked from Sam to Trey. "We owe you a great debt for saving the life of my impetuous young son." He threw a glance at Faunus, who lowered his head in shame.

"The humans should be thrown from the high cliffs!" Nikandros interrupted.

"I brought them here for punishment."

"Silence!" Silenus ordered, glaring at him. "You are too quick to believe all humans are our enemies." He turned back to Sam and Trey, his face clearing. "Why have you ventured upon our mountain where all humans fear to tread?" he asked. "Tell me the whole truth and we may be able to help you."

Trey heard Sam take a deep breath. "We're looking for part of the Warrior's Shield," she said. "And we're pretty sure it's in the mountain cave."

"What does this item look like?" asked Faunus, drawing close.

"We don't know exactly," said Sam. "Like a quarter of a big metal . . . shield, I suppose."

Trey tugged urgently at her sleeve. "Never mind that for the moment," he said. "Remember the serpent woman Michael mentioned? I've worked it out. It's Medusa."

"*The* Medusa?" gasped Sam, her eyes

like saucers. "I don't like the sound of that. How do we get the piece of the shield now?"

Trey shook his head. "I don't see how we can," he said. "I think we should go back home. We can't fight Medusa! It's crazy! Give me the disc – we need to go, now."

Sam leapt back before he could reach for the disc in her belt. "No!" she cried. "Not yet!" She wrapped her hands around her waist ... Then she froze, her eyes going wide ... "Oh no," she whispered.

Trey felt the energy drain out of his body. "It's gone, isn't it?"

In all the fighting, their only way home had disappeared. Trey stared at his cousin, the panic rising, almost choking him.

"You lost the disc!" he shouted, his voice shrill with fear. "We can't get home! What are we going to do now?"

11

BETRAYAL

"You should've put the disc in the backpack!" groaned Trey. "Where did you drop it?"

Sam shook her head. "I don't know," she said. "It could have fallen out anywhere." Trey forced himself to remember that only a few moments ago, she'd been passed out in a dead faint. This wasn't his cousin's fault.

He turned to Nikandros. "Did you see a metal disc, about ..." He held his hands fifteen centimetres apart. " ... this wide? Kind of grey. Covered in weird etchings? It's really important."

Nikandros shook his shaggy head.

"I saw it," said another of the satyrs, the one Trey remembered was called Pavlos.

"Brilliant!" gasped Sam. "Where is it?"

"One of the winged filth picked it up from the forbidden path before they fled," he told them.

"*Wha-a-a-at?*" screamed Sam. "You've gotta be kidding me! The harpies have got it?"

"Tell me of this disc," Silenus demanded.

"It's called the Heart of Light," explained Trey. "It's the centre of the Warrior's Shield."

"The Warrior's Shield belongs to the forces of Light," Sam broke in. "It got broken and the bits need to be found — that's why we are here. Medusa is sitting on one of the bits, and we need to get it off her."

Silenus leaned back, his brows lowered, his eyes half-closed.

"Thing is," Sam said. "We can't get home without the disc — so we really need to go up to the cave again." She gave Silenus a hopeful smile. "A little of that help you offered would be great."

Silenus nodded. "In gratitude for saving my son's life, we will help you," he said. "But it is folly to go to the cave in daylight. Medusa's serpents are drowsy at night, and the harpies sleep sound through the dark hours."

"That's great," said Trey. "But we're kind of on a deadline."

"You will rest here until the sun goes down," insisted Silenus. "Sleep will restore your strength. Then I will send my best fighters with you to the cave. They will help you to find those things you seek. But first . . ." He raised a hand just as Sam was opening her mouth to say something. "Eat and drink!"

Sam and Trey sat together on the grass, drinking cool water from wooden cups and picking at an assortment of nuts and fruits laid out around them in bowls. The sun was just dipping behind the mountains. Long cool shadows were spreading. Evening was gliding through the trees on soft, silken wings.

Some of the satyrs were playing instruments and dancing, but many sat in huddled groups, muttering among themselves and casting anxious or hostile glances at the two cousins. And apart from the ones who had given Sam and Trey food, none of the others had come anywhere near them. Then Nikandros peeled away from the group.

He was holding a bowl of yellowish fruit.

He bowed in front of them. "This is the food of heroes," he said, setting the bowl down between them. "Eat heartily – it will give you strength for this night's ordeal."

Sam turned to Trey, seeing him look as surprised as her. This wasn't like Nikandros. "Thanks," said Sam as he turned and strutted off. "Maybe this is his way of apologising," she muttered. She picked up a piece of fruit. "Apricots! I love apricots." She bit deeply and chewed. "Juicy sweet!" she mumbled. "Try one."

"No thanks," said Trey. "I'm too tired to think about eating."

Sam gurgled in delight as the thick, sweet juice ran down her throat. "You don't know what you're missing!" she spluttered, wiping her mouth and reaching for another.

"How long do you think we've been gone from the basement?" Trey asked her.

"A few hours," Sam said lazily, lying back in the lush grass. "Give or take."

"Mom will have missed us by now for sure," Trey said. "How are we going to explain where we've been?"

"Just tell her the truth," said Sam with a grin. "She'll be fine with it."

"I seriously doubt that," muttered Trey. "Hey – here comes Faunus."

Sam lifted her head, surprised at how

woozy she suddenly felt. There was a curious tingling in her fingertips and toes, and the glade seemed to swirl a little.

"My father will not let me come with you to Medusa's cave tonight," Faunus said despondently. "It is my punishment. Nikandros will lead the troop." He frowned. "I am sorry. I would like to have fought at your side again."

"No biggie," said Sam.

"Nikandros kind of hates our guts, doesn't he?" said Trey.

"Humans are not usually..." Faunus paused, as though struggling to find the right word, "... so *friendly* with we creatures of the forests." He finished with a shrug. "But you are different."

He smiled. "Good luck tonight. I will be thinking of you."

"Sam, are you ready?" Trey leaned over his cousin.

She sat up with a jerk, almost knocking him over. She'd fallen asleep and now she woke up full of energy. She bounded to her feet, twisting at the waist, punching the air. "Let's go get those harpies! I'm sick of hanging around here." She stared down at Trey in the gloom. "Come on – I wanna get some payback on those snakes. I wanna kick some asp!" She started laughing. "Kick some asp? Get it?"

Before Trey could tell his cousin to calm down, a heavy hand crashed down on his shoulder. Nikandros had come up behind him. "The sun is setting," he rasped. "The time has come. We must depart."

"But there's something wrong with Sam," Trey gasped, wincing at the way the satyr's fingers bored into his shoulder. "She's acting weird."

Nikandros ignored him. "We must leave now. It will be dark before we reach Medusa's cave."

Sam was bouncing on her toes, shadow-boxing. "I am so going to wipe the floor with those losers! Just let me at them!"

"You will meet your enemy soon

enough," Nikandros said with a cold smile.

Trey became more and more worried about Sam as they climbed through the forest in the gathering darkness. She was dancing around, kicking at nothing, punching the air, snorting and snarling like a boxer on their way to the ring.

Nikandros guided them silently out of the trees and on to the long, steep path that led to Medusa's cave. The night was strangely quiet, and not one of the ten satyrs that accompanied them had spoken a word from the moment they had left the glade.

Sam was the only one making any noise – muttering threats under her breath, kicking at tree trunks, chopping at branches.

Trey was getting a horrible feeling about what had happened to her.

Those apricots were drugged!

Not that he'd dare to accuse Nikandros to his face. And maybe it wasn't so bad? A fighting-mad Sam might be a real asset – just so long as she wasn't so out of it that she put herself in danger.

Nikandros stopped at the top of the pathway, lifting a hand.

Trey shuddered as he saw the mountain looming above them against the star-filled sky. The other satyrs gathered beside him, their spearheads glittering in the silvery light.

Sam stood right behind Nikandros, chattering to herself, fizzing with energy.

The cave mouth was a blot of darkness in the mountain wall.

Nikandros turned his amber eyes on Trey. "The serpent woman and the winged filth will be slumbering," he said in a low growl. "You and the other Chosen One must lead the way. We will be close behind. If Medusa awakes, we will engage her in battle while you seek the object you came here to find."

"Yes. Great. Thanks," stammered Trey, struggling against growing nerves. Nikandros's plan didn't make it sound as though the satyrs were going to fight alongside them – not in the way Silenus had promised. Now he could actually see the cave again – and remember what was inside – he was beginning to wish they'd told Michael to find some *other* Chosen Ones! But there was no turning back now.

"Sam? Are you ready for this?" Trey asked. "You remember the legend about Medusa, don't you? Whatever we do, we mustn't look into her eyes." Was his cousin even listening? She twitched and jerked her head impatiently.

"Yeah, yeah. Bring it on!" Sam growled.

"OK, come on then," murmured Trey. He gave a quick thumbs up to

Nikandros and the others, then stepped off the pathway.

He moved as silently as he could, trying to avoid his feet crunching down on any bones. The last thing they needed was to give the game away right at the very start.

Sam strode along at his side, her whole body quivering with suppressed energy.

They came to the yawning cave mouth. Trey paused, listening hard. Silence. Silence was good. Silence meant they were all probably fast asleep in there. He took a flashlight from his backpack, covering the end with a piece of thin cloth to keep the light at a minimum. They needed to be able to see – but they didn't want to shine a bright light into the eyes of a sleeping harpy.

"Ready?" he whispered to Sam.

"You bet!" She stepped into the cave. "Hey, Medusa!" she hollered at the top of her voice. "Suit up, lady! We're coming to get you!'

"No!" gasped Trey, grabbing at Sam as she ran into the cave.

Sam had wrecked their entire stealth plan! They needed backup – and they needed it right now.

He spun around, gesturing frantically towards the satyrs. But as Trey peered into the night, he saw no satyrs waiting at the head of the path. They had gone. All of them.

Trey heard hissing and shrieking echoing from the depths of the cave. Their enemies were awake – and Sam was running right into their lair.

12

THE FACE OF TERROR

Sam felt extraordinary. Her muscles seemed ready to burst out of her skin. Her blood rushed like fire through her veins. And she could see in the dark! How cool was that?

She glanced back, puzzled that Trey hadn't followed her.

Where was he?

Skulking out there in the dark! *Trey's no coward*, argued a small voice in her brain. *What are you doing? This is all wrong.*

Oh, shut it! Everything's cool.

She whipped around a corner, feeling fearless, brimming with power. She found herself in a great vaulted chamber, its high roof supported on thick pillars of natural rock. Several tunnels led off, winding away into deep darkness.

The floor was messy with more bones and with nasty-looking gobs and chunks of rotting flesh. The whole place reeked, but somehow Sam didn't mind the smell. It smelt like victory!

She strode into the middle of the chamber. She saw the glint and gleam of metal piled against the walls. Pieces of armour. Rusted weapons. Crumbling leather harnesses. Torn clothing. Bent and dented helmets. Stuff she guessed the harpies had stripped from the bodies of their vanquished foes. Swords. Spears. Shields.

Shields? Why did that ring a bell? Wasn't there something about a shield ... ?

She frowned, trying to think, but whatever memory the heaps of armour had ignited in her mind faded away again.

She was here to make Medusa cry like a little baby!

"Wakey-wakey!" she hollered, loving the way her voice bounced off the walls. She heard a creaky fluttering sound from above and looked up.

Harpies were hanging upside down from the ceiling, their wings folded around themselves like cocoons. Red eyes snapped open. Leathery pinions shook and spread. Mouths gaped, fangs gleaming between drawn-back lips.

And from one of the tunnels came the low hissing of snakes.

Medusa was waking up.

Hah! Think I'm scared of you?

Sam flung herself sideways as the harpies plummeted down towards her. She grabbed a sword from the heap, snarling as she swung it through the air.

The blade hit the nearest harpy with a meaty *thunk!* Sam grinned savagely as the winged creature tumbled yelling to the ground, blood spraying from a gaping wound. Another flew at her, claws stretched out, mouth open as though to bite her face off. Sam lifted her sword, aiming its point at the monster. She thrust the weapon between the gaping teeth. Gore splashed high as the blade sank deep into its throat. The harpy's body convulsed, ripping the hilt of the sword out of Sam's hands as it crashed headlong to the ground.

Sam sprang high into the air, snatching at the feet of another of the harpies. She caught a tight hold on them as she dropped down. The harpy twisted and thrashed, trying to free itself. But Sam's fingers were locked around the monster's ankles and she heaved back, all her weight on her heels. She twirled the harpy around like a living baseball bat, using it to swat the others out of the air.

All so easy! Where was Medusa? Now that was an enemy she could *really* prove herself against.

She grinned as she heard the hissing of snakes growing louder. She saw the creatures slithering from the darkness, eyes like black beads, tongues flickering.

A large figure emerged slowly from the gloom, cloaked and hooded, gliding forward on a river of writhing serpents. The cloak shimmered with scales and moved in rippling waves, as though hidden things were seething and squirming beneath. Sam could just glimpse the glint of a golden belt wrapped around a silver robe. Long fingernails stretched down from claw-like hands – perfect weapons. Medusa stood at least three metres tall. Sam narrowed her eyes, breathing hard, ready for anything.

"Well now, what have we here?" The voice was cracked, and simmering with menace.

"Gonna turn me to stone, are you?" Sam quivered with fearless anticipation, waiting for Medusa to come closer so she could strike. "Just you try it, lady!"

What are you talking about? screamed a voice in her head. *She totally will turn you to stone!* From the mouth of the cave she could hear another faint voice: "Sam! Where are you?" It was Trey. She'd finish what she'd come here to do, then she'd go and find her cousin.

"You have injured my harpies," said Medusa, anger flashing like a blade in her voice. "Who now will bring me my sweet morsels of food?" She glided across the cave floor, snakes still hissing around her. Sam felt one circling her ankle, and she angrily kicked it off.

That's it – just a little closer, lady!

Medusa lifted her hands to her head and drew back the cowl.

Sam winced, prepared for something horrible to be revealed.

But the gorgon was lovely. Shining, raven hair curled around a heart-shaped face. Green eyes gazed from under arched brows. A long, slender nose led to full, smiling lips.

"Oh!" Sam was taken aback. This she hadn't expected.

Medusa grinned. Long, thin, gappy teeth were revealed. Her eyes flashed like poisoned emeralds. Her hair rose about her head. Not hair. Snakes. Writhing snakes, black and filthy and disgusting.

Hideous.

Sam staggered as she stared into Medusa's terrible eyes, her limbs suddenly heavy, her mind slowing.

How did I get here? What's happening to me?

"Trey?" she croaked feebly. "Help ... me ..."

She stared down at her arms. They were crawling with flaking grey scabs,

like a fast-spreading, agonising rash chewing at her flesh. Legs like boulders. Too heavy to move. Eyes scratchy and dry. Lungs locking. Tongue frozen in her mouth. Muscles seizing up.

Turning ... to ... stone ...

The last thing she heard before her senses shut down completely was the sound of harsh, mocking laughter.

Trey froze as horrible noises echoed from deep in the mountain. Screaming. Fighting. Sam was in so much trouble in there. A new determination throbbed through him. He wasn't going to leave his cousin to face those monsters on her own.

He switched on the flashlight and ran into the cave.

"If Medusa shows herself, remember never to look in her face," he muttered to himself as he pounded down the long tunnel. "How was she killed in the story? It was Perseus, wasn't it? He cut her head off. But how did he get *close enough* to do that?" Then he remembered. "By looking at her reflection in his shield." He frowned. "We should have brought a mirror."

The sounds of fighting had died away.

His heart faltered. *They've killed Sam. I'm too late.*

The tunnel broadened out. Trey jogged to a halt, squeezing himself up against the wall, aiming the flashlight down at his feet so the beam wouldn't be seen by whatever was lurking in the darkness. Snakes, by all the hissing.

Many, many snakes.

He flicked a quick glance around the shoulder of rock. It was pretty dark, but he could make out crumpled shapes on the floor of what seemed to be a big cavern. The shapes were harpies. He couldn't see Sam.

"Beware, Chosen One!" The shock of the sudden voice almost shot him through the ceiling. He twisted his head and found himself staring into Faunus's amber eyes.

The satyr touched his finger to his lips and drew Trey away from the entrance to the chamber. "I will help you," whispered Faunus, his lips close to Trey's ear. "When I heard that Nikandros meant to abandon you to Medusa, I followed secretly." His eyes gleamed. "I will fight at your side, even if it means my death!"

"Sam's out of control," Trey whispered
back. "She ran in there on her own."

"She ate the Maenad fruit," said Faunus.
"It makes humans wild. When my father
hears of Nikandros's latest treachery ..."
He shook his head. "I am ashamed of
him and those who follow him."

"It's not your fault," Trey said. "And you're here now."

"I am your friend, Chosen One," growled Faunus, smacking his chest. "I will not betray you. What is your plan?"

"I don't have one," Trey admitted.

"What weapons do you bear?" asked Faunus.

"None, really," said Trey. "There's a penknife in my backpack. And I have a couple of flashlights." He shone the beam into the satyr's face. "Like this."

Faunus hissed and covered his eyes.

"Sorry," Trey said, averting the beam.

"No, it is good," said Faunus. "These creatures thrive in darkness – if you shine your light-stick in their faces, they will not be able to see."

"That's brilliant," said Trey, pulling his backpack off his shoulders and rummaging for the other flashlight.

"And while they are blinded, I can attack!" said Faunus, lifting his arm to show Trey his spear. "We will defeat them, my friend, and rescue your cousin!"

Trey switched on the second flashlight, its powerful beam raking the walls. He edged to the corner. "Don't look at Medusa's face," he reminded Faunus. Then he jumped out, flinging the first flashlight into the cavern. It bounced off the floor, its wide bright beam spinning over the roof and walls. He ran forward, aiming his other flashlight's beam, taking in the surprising scenc that opened up before him.

There were harpies strewn all over the floor. And quite a lot of fresh blood. None of the harpies were moving. Had Sam defeated the whole bunch of them single-handed?

Trey bounded over the fallen harpies, shining the beam deeper into the cavern. His heart almost stopped. The light flickered across a stone statue of a girl's silhouette. She had spiky hair. The statue had its back to him – but he knew immediately who it was.

"Sam!" he shouted in horror. "No!"

A tall, demonic form towered over the statue, clad in a glinting green cloak that floated on a myriad of writhing snakes. Trey glimpsed a face – but only for a split second before he turned his head away.

Medusa!

He felt the breeze of Faunus's spear as it whistled past his shoulder.

Trey heard the swipe of Medusa's arm, and the clattering of the spear as she batted it aside. Then she laughed — it was the coldest, cruellest sound Trey had ever heard.

A moment later, Medusa's cloak burst open and a whole host of snakes came flying out. They hurtled towards Trey, wrapping around him, jaws snapping, coils tightening around his limbs as he struggled to get free.

Trey heard a mocking voice above the mind-shredding hissing of the snakes.

"Another human," it jeered. "Another statue to adorn my lair." Trey felt himself being dragged across the ground – dragged towards the gorgon – his arms pinned as though by thick ropes, his breath cut off by a tightening noose of slimy scales around his throat.

13

MEDUSA'S LAIR

Trey strained against the coiling snakes, his brain ringing from their endless hissing as they closed around his body and throat. He kept his head turned to one side as he was pulled closer to the gorgon. He could see Faunus being dragged over too. After everything they'd been through, they'd lured their new friend back into danger.

The snakes squeezed tighter, hissing in his ear. He felt darkness rushing into his brain as the agony expanded in his chest.

Need. Air. Blackout. Soon. Any. Moment.

He concentrated every last drop of his strength to twist his wrist. There was only one last hope, if he could just ... He brought both hands together and wriggled around to shine the flashlight beam ... straight into Medusa's face. She let out a screech, as she slid backwards. She threw her arms up as snakes slithered from her sleeves. She fell to her knees and her snakes loosened their grip on Trey and writhed back towards her, hissing in terror.

Faunus leapt to his hooves and scrambled to retrieve his spear. He swiped the spearhead off the end of the staff, creating a makeshift knife he could wield faster, in close quarters. He sliced it through the air, back and forth, severing snake heads from bodies, hacking into their sinewy flesh. Then he stopped, and scrambled over to the pile of armour. Trey assumed he was looking for more weaponry.

Trey got shakily to his feet, his lungs still hurting, stars dancing before his eyes.

"Take this, Chosen One!" cried Faunus. "I found it among the armour."

Trey saw the satyr toss something high into the air. Something that shone silver as the flashlight beam caught it at the apex of its flight.

A curved, fan-shape of silvery metal!

Trey jumped and snatched the thing out of the air.

He knew straightaway what it was. A glittering piece of the Warrior's Shield. It was polished to a high shine, almost as reflective as a mirror. *A mirror ...* Trey thought.

Howling in rage, Medusa lunged forward, towering over him, her arms reaching out, her whole body a sickening mass of twisting snakes. "That is mine!" she screeched.

Almost without thinking, Trey held

thc shield fragment up so that its light shone into her eyes. She was forced to stare at her own poisonous gaze.

She threw her arms over her face, stumbling back, screaming. "No!" she cried. "This cannot happen!"

"Oh, yes it can," Trey muttered, a smile spreading across his face.

The hissing of the snakes rose to a terrible wail. Trey dropped to his knees, panting, wracked with pain, the flashlight wavering in his hand.

Something was happening to Medusa. A grey stain spread over her cloak. The flowing cloth stiffened, becoming rigid. The thrashing of the snakes slowed and halted, their bodies frozen, their mouths locked open, fangs turned to stone.

With shrinking eyes, Trey aimed his flashlight at Medusa's face. Her head was wrenched sideways on her neck, her mouth gaping, her eyes blank – lifeless.

Trey had turned her to stone with her own reflection. He'd done it!

All around him, stone snakes were scattered on the ground, twisted and coiled – caught for ever in their agonised death throes.

A creaking, cracking noise sounded at Trey's back. He turned. A spider's web of thin lines was creeping over the stone statue of Sam. A hand jerked. Her head flicked to one side, stone hair shaking out. Life and colour bled through the stone as Sam staggered forward.

"Oh, wow!" she gasped. "That was weird!"

Relief blazed through Trey. Sam was alive! With Medusa defeated, the spell of stone had been broken. He staggered to his feet, brandishing the shield fragment.

"We did it, cuz!" he yelled. "We totally did it!"

Faunus strode over, grinning from ear to hairy ear, spattered with blood and holding his spear high above his head. "Chosen Ones, indeed!" he said, his eyes glowing. "This victory will ring down the centuries!"

"How? What? Where?" Sam stared around herself. "What happened?"

Trey smiled. "You were drugged. You

got a bit overexcited. You came in here to fight Medusa by yourself and she turned you to stone. You looked into her eyes, didn't you?"

"Er . . . " Sam rubbed her forehead. "Um, maybe."

Trey laughed. "It doesn't matter. Faunus and I rescued you." He shook the shield fragment between his hands, holding it up like the trophy at the Super Bowl. "And we found this!"

"Will you return to your home, now that your mission is fulfilled?" asked Faunus.

"Yes," said Trey. "As soon as we find the Heart of Light." He aimed his flashlight around the room, picking out the piles of rusty armour. "I really hope it's here. Otherwise we're in big trouble."

"Chillax, cuz!" said Sam. "I see it!"

She bounded across the cavern and picked up the disc from the side of one of the fallen harpies. "Who kicked *their* scruffy butts?" she asked, looking around. "Someone really went to town on them!"

"That would be you," said Trey.

"Cool!" Sam came back to where Trey and Faunus were standing.

Trey eyed Medusa thoughtfully. Even turned to stone, she was pretty awesome. "One thing puzzles me," he said. "The myths say she was killed by a guy called Perseus."

"So?" shrugged Sam. "They got it wrong."

An ominous creaking rang out. Trey stared in alarm as hair-thin cracks began to race up the sides of Medusa's cloak.

"Unless she's only been turned to stone temporarily," he cried, backing away from the great stone gorgon. "It looks like she's still alive in there!"

The cracks widened. A few snake heads began to twitch.

"We're out of here!" yelled Sam. "Faunus – hoof it! She's waking up."

"It has been an honour to fight at your side," said the satyr, bowing low.

"Likewise," said Sam. "Now – get out of here!"

Faunus raced off, his hooves clattering on the cave floor. At the entrance, he paused and turned back round, lift-ing his spear once more in salute before vanishing around the corner.

Sam held out the Heart of Light. "Quick, grab it!"

Trey caught hold of the disc, gripping the fragment of the shield tight with his other hand. No way was he letting *that* go!

"On my mark," shouted Sam. "Three. Two. One. Break!"

Trey pressed down on the disc. It felt warm in his grasp. Something slithered over his shoulder. There was a hiss. A cracked voice shouted, "Die, human filth!"

An electric shock of pain ran up his arms. There was a loud crack like trapped thunder, and a blue-white lightning flash . . .

. . . and they were back in the basement.

"Wow! Head-rush!" gasped Sam, almost toppling over.

Michael was standing by the basement stairs, tall and serene.

Trey wobbled towards him, holding out the quarter of the Warrior's Shield. "We rescued it," he gasped.

Michael smiled. "Do not give it to me, Chosen One," he said gently. "It is not permitted for me to touch it."

"Oh, sorry." Trey gazed down at the curved face of the quarter-circle. "Hey, Sam – look at this," he gasped.

He held the shiny piece of metal flat

between them. Sam leaned over and saw that the contours of a face were etched into it. A heart-shaped face with a snarling mouth filled with needle-sharp teeth, and with hair that writhed like ...

"Snakes," she breathed, amazed. "It's Medusa. That is so cool!"

"Find a safe place to keep it," Michael said. "You have done well, Chosen Ones."

"It was a piece of cake," Sam replied. "Nothing to it!"

Michael frowned as he looked at her.

"What?" she asked. "OK, it got a bit hairy now and then. But nothing we couldn't handle."

Michael lifted his hand, his finger pointing to her forehead. "You have the mark of Light, Chosen One," he said. "The crescent moon."

Sam touched the curved wound above her left eyebrow.

"How come I don't get a mark of Light?" asked Trey. "What am I, the sidekick?"

"You totally are," laughed Sam. "I'm gonna call you Robin from now on."

"You are equals," said Michael. "But not all bear the mark." He turned to Trey. "Hide the shield now. Someone comes."

Trey nipped across the basement and tucked the fan-shaped piece of metal into an old cardboard box.

"How long were we gone?" Sam asked Michael. "What time is it?" She looked up at the narrow basement window. It was light outside. Was it tomorrow already? That would take some explaining!

"You were gone only for a brief time," Michael said. "No more than a fraction of your day."

"Wicked!" said Sam. "We were there for hours. It was night and everything. How's that work?"

Trey rolled his eyes. "Time moves more slowly there," he said. "*Obviously!*"

"Rest now," said Michael. "Eat. Sleep. Tomorrow will bring new labours."

"I know. We have to find the next piece of the Warrior's Shield," said Trey. "Where will we go?"

Footsteps sounded above them and there was the creak of the basement door being opened.

"Kids?" Trey's mother's voice rang down the stairs. "I've made pizza. Come and get it."

Sam looked to where Michael had been standing, but he was gone.

"Coming, Mom," Trey called, gesturing frantically at Sam to put her half of the disc away.

"I don't know what you kids found to do down there all afternoon!" called Aunt Jenn. "You should go outside — get some fresh air into your lungs!"

Sam and Trey poked their halves of the disc away under some blankets. Sam nudged her cousin in the ribs as they made for the stairs. "Shall I tell her what we've been doing, or will you?" she said.

He looked at her. "Let's sleep on it, oh *Chosen One*," he said. "I think we're going to have enough trouble explaining where you got that cut from!"

Sam used her fingers to comb her hair

down over her eyes. "That can wait!" she said. "Hey!" She caught hold of his sleeve. "Considering all the fighting and running about and freaking out we've been doing, we should feel totally shattered." She looked at him. "*Do* you feel totally shattered?"

"Now you mention it, no," said Trey. "Do *you*?"

"No, I feel fine," she replied.

"Maybe the Heart of Light has restorative powers?" said Trey.

Sam blinked at him. "Cool!" she said.

"Are you two coming, or not?" called Trey's mother.

"We'll be right there, Aunt Jenn!" shouted Sam as they ran up the stairs. The tantalising smell of fresh-baked pizza wafted over them. Trey's mum held the door wide. Sam turned, pausing for a moment, gazing at the basement.

What next? she wondered. Where was the second piece of the Warrior's Shield – and what kind of trouble would they get themselves into finding it?

THE END

ARE YOU A
GREEK GEEK?

A lot of the story in *Medusa's Curse* was influenced by real mythological details. If you ...

SAM: I'm gonna have to stop you right there. Everyone knows that there's nothing "real" about mythical creatures. They're myths – made up, stories, fairy tales. Get my drift?

All right, all right. You don't have to be so pedantic.

TREY: Hey, did you know that the word

"pedantic" (which means "picky", by the way) derives from a French word, which itself was derived from an Italian word ... and that Italian word was derived from a Latin word – which has its origins in a *Greek* word? Phew!

Um, okay. Thanks for that. It's obvious you two pay attention at school. Moving on, we've pulled together a little multiple choice quiz.

SAM AND TREY: A quiz! Awesome!

Err, it's not for you. It's for the readers.

SAM: Oh . . .

Disappointed?

SAM: No. Of *course* not . . .

THE GREEK
GEEK QUIZ

QUESTION ONE

Which of these was a favourite trick of harpies?

A. Defecating on enemies from a great height

B. Shoving custard pies into enemies' faces

C. Drowning their enemies

SAM: I'd hardly call drowning a "trick"!

The answer is . . .

A: By defecating on them from a great height. Or so legend has it.

TREY: That's disgusting! Hey, did you know that the oldest known example of a dessicated poo is more than 14,300 years old and found in Oregon City, California?

SAM: Moving on . . .

QUESTION TWO

What were the names of Medusa's gorgon sisters?
  A. Tracy and Sandra
  B. Stheno and Euryale
  C. Zeus and Troy

The answer is . . .

B: Stheno and Euryale

SAM: Stheno had red snakes for hair and Euryale was famous for her ability to give ear-splitting cries. She probably would have done well on *The X-Factor*!

TREY: Unlike her sisters, Medusa was mortal – which might explain why she seemed to be the angriest!

QUESTION THREE

Which era followed the Neolithic period?

   A. The Stone Age
   B. The Ice Age
   C. The Bronze Age

The answer is …

C: The Bronze Age

SAM: That's what it says in our reference books, but in other parts of the world people refer to a "Copper Age" before reaching the "Bronze."

QUESTION FOUR

Which Greek god was Silenus said to have tutored?

  A. Ares

  B. Poseidon

  C. Dionysus

The answer is . . .

C: Dionysus

SAM: Wasn't Dionysus meant to be god of wine and parties, and that sort of thing?

TREY: Hmm – I can't picture those two

getting along, either. But maybe Silenus mellowed after we left!

QUESTION FIVE

In Ancient Athens, how would a family announce the birth of a baby daughter?

A. By painting a pink cross on their front door

B. By pinning sheep's wool to their front door

C. By posting a written notice on their front door

The answer is ... *B: By pinning sheep's wool to their front door*

SAM: Well, that's slightly more civilised than what would happen to some baby girls in this period. I've read that unwanted girls were left in a public place, where they would either die, or be "adopted" by a passer-by ... who would usually put them to work as a slave!

QUESTION SIX

In Sam and Trey's adventures, you've heard of Gondwana — but what was the name of the other supercontinent which existed hundreds of millions of years ago?

A. Laurasia

B. Pangaea

C. Pannotia

The answer is ...

A: Laurasia

TREY: Most of what we now call the northern hemisphere was once Laurasia. Amazing to think about, isn't it?

Knowledge certainly is power, isn't it? How would Sam and Trey have fared on their "raid" if they hadn't brushed up on their history? Hopefully they'll read up on the other cultures that Michael is going to send them to. But where will their next adventure take place ...?

COMPETITION TIME!

Answer this bonus question for a chance to win some special Myth Raiders goodies.

What were the names of Medusa's parents?

A. Pegasus and Chrysaor
B. Phorcys and Ceto
C. Scylla and Ladon

To enter the competition go to
www.mythraiders.co.uk
and fill in your details.

You can also send your entry by post to:
Myth Raiders Competition
Hachette Children's Books, Carmelite House,
50 Victoria Embankment
London, EC4Y 0DZ

The competition is open to UK and Republic of Ireland residents only. Go to the website for full details plus terms and conditions.

CLOSING DATE: 30/04/2016

ABOUT THE AUTHOR

A. J. Hunter is the pen name for two authors, Allan and James, who bonded over their shared love of mythical creatures. After poring over their history books and trawling through the Internet, Myth Raiders was born! When they're not thinking up new adventures for Sam and Trey, they can usually be found indulging one of their many interests, such as practicing kung fu, growing beards, writing fantasy novels for Young Adults, helping develop apps and selling flowers in Covent Garden market. But which hobby belongs to which author? Only A. J. Hunter knows the answer to that . . .